Introspection Of Inner Thoughts And Prespective About Life

Karan Sharma

Ukiyoto Publishing

All global publishing rights are held by

Ukiyoto Publishing

Published in 2023

Content Copyright © Karan Sharma

ISBN 9789360160043

All rights reserved.
No part of this publication may be reproduced, transmitted, or stored in a retrieval system, in any form by any means, electronic, mechanical, photocopying, recording or otherwise, without the prior permission of the publisher.

The moral rights of the author have been asserted.

This book is sold subject to the condition that it shall not by way of trade or otherwise, be lent, resold, hired out or otherwise circulated, without the publisher's prior consent, in any form of binding or cover other than that in which it is published.

www.ukiyoto.com

I dedicate this book to my mother Mrs Rubina Sharma and my aunty Mrs Amita Das.

Contents

Chapter 1	1
Chapter 2	2
Chapter 3	3
Chapter 4	4
Chapter 5	5
Chapter 6	6
Chapter 7	8
Chapter 8	9
Chapter 9	10
Chapter 10	12
Chapter 11	13
Chapter 12	15
Chapter 13	16
Chapter 14	17
Chapter 15	19
Chapter 16	20
Chapter 17	21
Chapter 18	22
Chapter 19	23
Chapter 20	25
Chapter 21	26
Chapter 22	27
Chapter 23	28
Chapter 24	29
Chapter 25	30
Chapter 26	31
Chapter 27	32
Chapter 28	33

Chapter 29	34
Chapter 30	35
Chapter 31	36
Chapter 32	37
About the Author	*38*

Chapter 1.

The journey of life is full of mystery, which is waiting to be explored by true seekers. The definition of life full of positivity, love, kindness, humility and gratitude depends upon the perception of an individual depending upon time, place and circumstances of that person. It's not necessary that materialistic accumulation of modern lifestyle can give us a long term happiness. There are few individuals who keep justifying their point using their logic of perception. However, there are chances that unnecessarily accumulating things more than our needs can open the door of hankering for more accumulation of things which can neither quench our greed nor can make us genuinely feel happy and contented during our entire lifetime. The current global situation being in a turmoil of pandemic only portrays the fact that we as humans have highly developed but at the cost of true human values. The current human values are based on the platform of greed, anger, lust and envy which has truly taken a toll on our intellectual, emotional and mental health. Within a span of few decades, there are also instances of demeaning act act of humans which is the basic reason for raising a big question about our existence and the survival of future generations. It's necessary for a collective effort of raising the mindset, which is required in current global scenario. We need to understand the true values of humanity which is essential for our civilization and the world in a long run where there is an aura of love, kindness, gratitude and humility all around.

Chapter 2

The definition of life and all events are a mirror reflection of various thoughts and actions of every individual. Depending on those thoughts people try and work to emancipate and liberate themselves from previous unpleasant experience or state of being underprivileged. In this flow of making our lives smooth we often mould our mindset to get a sense of abundance which includes happiness, money, social status and fame. But, in this race of creating a sense of abundance we mostly overlook the basic fact that real happiness is an outcome of invoking a sense of gratitude for all we possess. We need to understand the fact that any thought which assists to invoke a sense of false ego can only falter our basic human nature. As a matter of fact we humans, are social animal cannot afford to retain the sense of false ego, envy, greed and lust. But, it can be replaced by right effort, right attitude, right consciousness, right speech and right action. In today's fast paced society, it's really essential that we as humans make a collective effort to be a better person, so that a better world is created for our future generations where love will prevail in every action and phase of life.

Chapter 3

Our modern society has been equipped with bouquet of information which has always emphasised in developing oneself with a sense of acquiring excess of everything that has a limited capability of giving a sense of superficial happiness and fulfillment. The race to acquire " superficial happiness" has indeed robbed the society of it's basic essence of love, kindness, gratitude and happiness which is essential in a long run to sustain the basic effort to make our world a living paradise, where everyone is equal irrespective of caste, creed, gender, nationality, skin colour or socio economic background. But the demeaning thought process of our modern society due to obvious reasons has only helped to create a sense of insecurity and frustration to such an extent that there is a rise of all sorts of actions which potrays a horrific instinct within humans which is even worse than animals. Such actions come into spotlight through different channels which compels us to think and introspect our true human instinct and the true reason of our existence. As a matter of fact, currently our world is enveloped in a chaotic aura which is a result of demeaning thought process like anger, greed, envy, lust, physical and emotional abuse of women and children and hunger for power/money and status. Every such thought gives rise to another thought like:- being envious/angry of others prosperity gives rise to greed for power/status/money, by achieving power/status/money gives rise to exploit women and the weaker section either physically or mentally. At this point there is a high possibility of humanity losing it's real purpose and forgetting it's reason of existence. It's really necessary for every member of society to check their thought process and be responsible individual to make this world a better and a happier place.

Chapter 4

Every perception towards life is a mirror reflection of one's own individuality. The individual mindset depends upon the company or association one keeps in their lifetime to sustain themselves in social arena. But, it depends upon one's own free will, whether one wishes to absorb the goodness or willingly follow the vice of their association. Generally, in today's fast paced society people bankrupt of their time and consideration to analyse one's own emotional and social needs. Moreover, there is a notion on the basis of perception that one can be happy after attaining material things that are incapable of providing long term happiness. We as humans need to sincerely realise that real happiness and contentment is within ourselves. We need to find it within ourselves by invoking the dormant essence of kindness, love and gratitude. It's on the basis of such subtle nature that we can realise the real essence of happiness and contentment and can create an example for our future generations to follow the same path of kindness, love and gratitude. So that the world becomes a happier place to live and every individual experience the heavenly bliss of ultimate happiness and contentment.

Chapter 5

In today's fast paced life, we forgotten the basic fact that human life is an opportunity to appreciate the creation of nature and our planet. The perception of life differs from person to person depending upon one's own intellectual level and the company one keeps. Moreover, in recent times we have been self motivated to accept the notion that true happiness or the sense of fulfillment can be obtained by hankering over the possession of external objects. It's not necessary that hankering over external things for short term happiness is always money. Apart from money there are few individuals who easily get carried away and get superficially attracted to the desire of possessing beautiful women, intoxication, luxurious lifestyle, lavish parties or simply being megalomania. There are few platforms in which discussions are done to melow down these types of outrageous thought process which can deviate us from the true purpose of our valuable human life. Humans, being one of the most intelligent creation of nature, have the responsibility to make our planet a happier and a healthier place so that the rays of positivity reaches every sphere of our thought process and help to do some constructive actions. Unfortunately, we as humans and the society have become a slave of our own perverted senses and have made our own life very complicated. Presently, the global situation is just the mirror reflection of own mindset and actions and as a result there is chaos in the name of skin colour, nationality, ethnicity, gender, socio economic condition, religious or political viewpoint. We ourselves are to be blamed for the effort of degrading our thought process to the extent of manipulating the essence of our real purpose of life. We ought to raise our level of consciousness to the extent of realisation of equality between all humans on the foundation of unbiased love and respect for all irrespective of caste, creed, skin colour, nationality, ethnicity or socio economic background.

Chapter 6

The fire of curiosity keeps burning in every person which inspires him/her to look beyond the obvious and work according to the intensity of their curiosity to know and evaluate their thoughts, actions, needs and necessity. At different phases of civilization there had been thinkers, philosophers and motivators who had been like a torch bearer for the rest of society to show the path of utilizing their curiosity to have a positive effect in their life and in our human society. As a result there had been many such people who had excelled in their respective fields for the welfare of society. But, as the time kept going and the modern society has been in the race to gain material benefits, the effort to utilize the curiosity in a positive direction has been fading and covered with a blanket of satisfying the senses which has eventually twisted the real purpose of life. It's essential to understand our true purpose of life and utilizing our thoughts, actions and curiosity to the welfare of our fellow beings. Few people may justify their opinion by giving their own example to gain material benefits on the basis of their logic of perception. But hardly do they make a sincere effort to look at life as it is, which is perhaps meant to spread love, kindness, gratitude and knowledge which is beneficial for everyone in a long run. Moreover, as an individual without any partiality we can observe that there are many instances in life where people usually portray their perverted mindset which is covered in the name of "Modern Mindset". However, the so called " Modern Mindset " is usually a mix of various such physical , mental, emotional , financial, religious, political frustration. All these chaos in one's life has the capability to determine the fact about the current global scenario and the tendency to exploit others in the name of getting happiness and satisfaction. Unless there is a change in our mindset from the grass root level , there are bleak chances of witnessing any changes in world which will be beneficial for everyone along with a sense of equality among all humans irrespective of caste, creed, gender, nationality, socio – economic background, religious belief and skin colour. To have a better world we need to change our mindset and to change our mindset we need to change our approach towards life and our surrounding which is need of the hour.

Chapter 7

The quality of modern lifestyle is a result of a multi layered confusion of mind, which is unable to differentiate between the ' Needs' and ' Wants' of an individual. On the basis of this confusion people usually define the meaning of happiness, fulfillment and contentment. But , rarely there is a sincere effort to explore and know the difference between " Needs" and " Wants" . As the modern society is being constantly invaded with technically advanced products there has been a great deficit of fine sense of judgement which is essential each and every individual for a higher purpose of life. As an humans we have our own share of needs which includes physical, emotional, intellectual, social and economical. Moreover, nature has been very kind to fulfill all these needs for each one of us. However, opposite to that, there are a certain section of people who lack the capability to acknowledge this basic fact and often change and mix the essence of their " Needs " and " Wants " by using their perverted sense of logic and eventually end up in physical, emotional, economical and social frustration. As a result of these types of frustration we have come across many such instances where there have been cases of ghastly and outrageous crimes against women and society which has raised indeed raised questions about such mindset and has also helped to showcase the lack of respect of individuality of others specially women. We nees to understand that all our physical, emotional,social and economical needs are limited and if we choose wisely and work accordingly to fulfill our needs then our world will be a much better place where love and respect for every individual will prevail. But, if we choose and become the slaves of our unlimited and towering " Needs " then we will be solely responsible to envelope the world in the darkness of negativity of anger, lust, envy, greed and the tendency to exploit others specially women. It's our choice whether we embrace the light of right knowledge and wish to fulfill our " Needs " or jump into the never ending fire of our " Wants " and turn our beautiful life into a burning hell.

Chapter 8

In this fast paced world, every individual is self motivated to be desirous to achieve their never ending aspirations to achieve a life full of all types of luxuries which includes excessive accumulation of material things. In this race of accumulation, we have voluntarily desolated ourselves from our true selves and our true purpose of life. Moreover, we have moulded our mindset in such a way that we perceive every phase of life, desires and relationships in such a manner that it only assists to make us feel restless and miserable. The development which we see all around us is just a reflection of what we perceive and we assume that it can give us everlasting happiness, joy and a sense of fulfillment. But, hardly we dedicated some time or taken any initiative to look within ourselves and work upon our thoughts, actions or speech which is the main cause of all sorts of chaos including hatred, jealousy, envy, ego and lust. On the basis of such demeaning thought process our so called " Modern Society " is in the grip of being a living example of "Dual Personality" which thinks it to be a normal phenomenon of thinking in one way and using our free will of using our actions and speech differently. As a result, the true essence of love, kindness, gratitude, compassion and mutual trust has lost it's value in our life. We need to be cautious of our thought, actions and speech which has the power to make this world a better place where there is no room for any type of chaos which can erode the essence and meaning of our true purpose of life.

Chapter 9

The journey of life is full of various experience which gives us an opportunity to know go through ups and downs of different phases in life. The outcome of those experiences can either have a positive or a negative impact in our everyday life and as well as our thought process. But, in this process we as humans have overlooked or skipped to evaluate and know our true self and be humble enough to celebrate the positive aspect of our life. In every civilization, there are many such festivals which gives us a message and teaches us to acknowledge the essence of positivity in life which can create a balance of mind and emotions and also empower us intellectually for a strong aura of love, compassion, respect and kindness. But our so called " civilised" " modern " and " educated " society has diverted the true essence of all such teachings. Since, last few years we have been witnessing and participating in celebrating " Women's Day " around the world to acknowledge and show express our appreciating the feminine energy. Although the initiative of celebrating Womanhood is a noble way of expressing our gratitude to the feminine energy, but unless there is a collective effort to eliminate the evil of dogmatic approach towards women in the name of social or religious taboo and objectify her to satisfy one's lustful desires and aspire to exploit her mentally and physically our society cannot be free from the shackles of of an unhealthy aura of maniacs and rigid patriarchal mindset. Most of the great religions of the world have held women in high esteem, but with the flow of time few section of society have infected the general psyche of others with their perverted mindset and approach towards women in a very lustful manner and have also set up a mindset to see or objectify women or girl child as a medium to satisfy their evil intentions. Unless, we change our approach and change our mindset the real purpose of celebrating " Women's Day " will never be justified. When the society is a safer place for women where she is not judged based on the basis of her clothes, habits and status and neither she is exploited financially, emotionally or physically then the true meaning of celebrating Womanhood will be justified.

Chapter 10

Life is like a garden which blossoms as per the effort of an individual. Though, tending to the needs of this garden of life life is not an easy task, but it is indeed a challenge which we as an individual need to accept and work upon our perspective and our actions so that the fragrance and aura of love, compassion, kindness and gratitude prevails around us. As a matter of fact every effort has an equal and opposite reaction, where the scope of resistance is high. But it depends upon our will power and intention which determines whether the quality of our precious life takes a diversion towards a positive way or it gets degraded and makes us a slave of our senses and unfulfilled aspirations. We as humans need to acknowledge and accept the fact that every individual is an unique creation of nature and has been blessed with some intensity of positivity. As the essence of individuality prevails in everyone of us, we need to strongly have a positive approach towards anyone we come across in the journey of life and respect each other's individuality. Unless there is a collective effort to make our life meaningful and blissful there are fair chances of our life being enveloped by a perineal chaos which may effect us mentally, intellectually or physically. Hence it's time to wake up for us and refrain ourselves from being a slave of our senses and make a sincere effort to work and blossom the garden of our life and fill it with the fragrance of pure love for everyone irrespective of caste, creed, nationality, skin colour, socio economic background or religious affiliation.

Chapter 11

Festivals are an integral part of human life which is full of hidden meaning and teaches us the way to harmonize with our true self and nature. Every culture around the world have their own way to celebrate their festivals within the frame work of their own religion which is in accordance with different seasons of the year. Similarly, the festival Holi which is celebrated in India has something to teach us as an individual and as a society. As it's popularly known that Holi is a festival of colour and it's celebrated by applying colour on each other followed by exchanging different type of sweets. However, the main essence of the festival is to enlighten us and to make us acknowledge that applying of colour symbolizes the presence of unconditioned love and respect in our heart in the mode of sweetness for each other irrespective of cast, creed, nationality , skin colour or socio economical background. We as an individual need to understand the basic fact that human life is precious and it is meant to be lead in a constructive manner for the welfare of self and society with love, respect, humility and kindness in our heart. Unfortunately, a certain section of society have always taken the initiative to leave no opportunity to degrade the very essence of a festival like Holi and trying to implement their perverted mindset which is highly contaminated with anger, lust, greed, hatred and all sorts of actions which can only demean humanity. The collective effort to initiate and to understand the basic human tendency and our true self is an art and it's necessary in current times to colour the canvas of our inner self with love, compassion, kindness, humility and gratitude. So that there is an abundance of mutual trust within fellow human beings. The current situation around the world is a reflection of unfulfilled human aspirations which is alloyed with varied emotions to implement one's own desires and to satisfy the hunger for excessive need of power, wealth, social status, and recognition. One other hand there are few people who take the initiative to acknowledge the fact and try to be humble in their own capacity and work for the welfare of self and society on humanitarian grounds. Any good deed done without expectation and attachment is a medium through which the blank canvas of our heart can be filled with colours of love, empathy, kindness and humility. However, it's not late enough to understand and acknowledge our true purpose of life and spread the colour of humanity throughout the world and contribute in a positive way to spread the message of pure love.

Chapter 12

Since the dawn of civilization knowledge has been a guiding star for human society to lit the lamp of curiosity within us and to make a sincere effort to enlighten our intellect and have a rendezvous with our true self. Great thinkers and philosophers had played a crucial role to make us understand our true nature and the purpose of our existence either by their eternal teachings. As our society progressed in every field, the ability to acknowledge and practicing those teachings took a backseat and has eventually converted us from being the seeker of true knowledge to an individual full of hypocrisy and the tendency to exploit others either financially or mentally and physically. As a result there has been a lot of chaos which is prevailing around the world which has effected everyone irrespective of caste, creed, gender, skin colour, nationality or socio economic background. The motivation factor which is present in everyone of us has taken a diversion in a different path and we can find that mostly we are surrounded by people who are hypocrites in their own way and are living example of their duality of mind and thoughts. Their mindset can only see the twisted meaning of every emotion or action. Hardly there are few individuals who work upon themselves and try to find their true purpose of life and individuality of soul. Global peace can only be achieved when we as a society and individual make an honest initiative to acknowledge and accept the true knowledge of self and practice to lead a life which is enveloped with love, kindness, humility and gratitude towards all our fellow beings and set our thoughts free from the shackles of duality of our mind and embrace the individuality of self and others irrespective caste, creed, nationality,skin colour etc.. By embracing the individuality of our fellow beings we can contribute in a humble way for Love, Peace and Joy prevail around the world.

Chapter 13

The current mindset of our modern society is a mirror reflection of highly inflated ego under the influence of false pride which has detoriated the quality of precious human life and intellect. The essence of false ego often reflected in every thought, action and lifestyle. There is indeed a fast depreciation of thoughts and actions which is one of the reason of distress for others and self. The need to satisfy one's superficial desire and to perceive others and our external situation is also the outcome of perverted mindset due to the upbringing or past experience of few individuals. Moreover, in this dilemma it's really difficult to know the difference between our basic human instinct and the desire to flow with the desires of our egoistic self which is drenched in false pride. It's essential to know our true purpose of existence and the importance of unalloyed love, compassion and kindness for our fellow beings and nature. Absence of our true human qualities have given rise to ghastly acts of mistreating our own fellow beings either emotionally, physically, intellectually or financially. Hence, it's high time that we know and realise our true self and be responsible human beings to work towards global peace with due respect , kindness and humility for every form of life.

Chapter 14

Emotions are the basic force which motivates every human to determine his / her way to lead their life. It depends upon everyone of us to choose the path of either elevating ourselves to a level of love, compassion, kindness, gratitude and humility or get sucked into the negativity of hatred, anger, jealousy, lust or envy which itself has the capability to ruin the peace of mind and degrade the quality of an individual life. In recent times there has been few instances where the portrayal of a perverted mindset had been clearly visible in our human society in the form of various incidents like exploitation of weaker section of society. In this process of exploitation women and children had bore the brunt of social and religious dogmatism in the form of emotional or physical torture. Though there had been social outrage against the ghastly acts towards women but the solution of this problem is still far from reach. Unless there is a clear intention to educate the patriarchal society through proper mode of education or by giving an opportunity to raise the level of consciousness it will be a difficult task to protect the dignity of women either in home or in professional level. The other aspect of this mindset is that there has been a lack of proper atmosphere and guidance to train the young mind to analyze the ill effects of having the tendency to exploit human life specially the fairer skin. As it is a general thought that women are only made to serve the family and give birth and raise children The excessive exposure to few unsolicited sites and printed material has lowered the mindset to such a level that it has become a common notion to perceive women to be an object to satisfy natural urges. Moreover, whenever there is a little scope of diverting our mind there is a bombardment of such illicit materials which results in withdrawal of natural human instinct. We as humans need to understand the basic fact that the feminine energy in form of women is the foundation of a healthy human society. If there is proper respect and love with an essence of gratitude and humility then the world will be a healthier place to live. Women are indeed the best creation of nature that if given equal opportunity can make a healthy society where there is equal opportunity for everyone to prosper. It's the need of the hour to acknowledge the true essence of feminine energy in our life and around us.

Chapter 15

Every form of life has a meaning and purpose for every living entity. We all as a living being are bound to journey through life within the framework of nature's law. However , we as humans being the most advanced version of nature's creation are blessed with higher intellect and the ability to explore the unknown for the welfare of everyone. Since the dawn of civilization human society is being empowered with knowledge of self and nature which had been essential for elevating the intellectual capability of everyone. But the flow of time has bought us to a threshold where there is a state of confusion and dilemma to know the difference between practical approach towards life and materialistic paraphernalia. The reflection of such confusion is prevalent in our modern society, where there is an aura of hypocrisy, elevated ego, false pride, urge to satisfy the senses or lust and the a never ending effort to gain money, power and fame more than required. The concept of being contented, being happy and acknowledging the Divinity in every being and learning to be truthful with oneself has taken a back seat and are also being regarded as backdated or the height of rigidity. In recent times we have come to know about many such instances which are bound to raise a question about the purpose of our existence. In modern times, we need to understand that education is necessary for all but if it is not utilized for the welfare of others or it doesn't make us a better person then the whole concept of being educated is at question. It's really necessary in today's fast moving world to realize the fact that every experience is an outcome of our action, and every action is an outcome of our thought. So to have a good experience we need to have a sound and matured mind which is trained to refrain from any sort of negativity which can harm us and our environment. Money, Fame or Social Status can be good for an individual if it is earned with a good and pure intention and utilized for the making the world a happier and healthier place for the our next generation.

Chapter 16

Leading a peaceful life with an essence of humility and gratitude has been a great challenge in today's so called " modern " and " civilised" society. Perception of leading a peaceful life depends upon the mindset of different people. It's a general notion that modern education system is the foundation of a civilized and modern society. But , unless there is a way to train the mind and walk in the path to invoke our true human essence, the use of such education will be of no use. In last few decades we have seen the effort to excel in gathering information about various subjects which is useful for assimilating the idea of accumulating excessive of material objects and be voluntarily blindfolded to acknowledge the true purpose of existence. Moreover, excessive accumulation of material things are the foundation for degrading our overall thought process. As an individual we need to be proactive and make a sincere effort to train our mind and use our life in a positive manner. We ought to to understand that create an aura of happiness and positivity around the world, we need to change our perception and be the lamp to spread the light of love, humility and gratitude and acknowledge the presence of people who are reciprocal to our sincere efforts.

Chapter 17

The human mind being a store house for various thoughts and emotions is the foundation of current scenario globally. Many thoughts are often being controlled by our own materialistic and selfish desires which are unable to give happiness and bliss in a long run. The thoughts which are the predominant factor in our mind and life are highly motivated to perceive every action or situation around us in such a way that it can only temporarily give us a sensual satisfaction. The modern society has no doubt become a slave of such thoughts and has accepted it to be reality. Emotions like love, gratitude, kindness, humility and tolerance has taken a backseat and are often portrayed as a sign of weaker people. Unfortunately, there is a misconception in our society that excessive of wealth, false ego and pride are the signs of prosperity in modern world and to survive there has to be a competition in every level. But in this mode of misconception there is a fair chance of overlooking the actual essence of true humanity which if full of love, kindness, gratitude and humility. It's a dilemma that a certain section of people are trying to convince others about the misconception of being wealthy. However, there is no harm in being wealthy unless it's not harming anyone. But the actual challenge is to be rich. The concept of being rich is not associated with accumulating money or gold, but it's about accumulating excessive love, humility and kindness with an essence of grace and also being untouched by any sort of negativity. The world needs to understand that there is ample opportunity to explore true love but there is hardly any sincere effort to spread the light of true love. Our precious human life is being robbed of it's true nature and forcibly made pregnant with envy, jealousy, hatred, false pride, ego and lust. Indulgence in such lower level of thoughts in any form has indeed made our world a place of various conflicts. We as humans need to raise our consciousness and reach to a level of maturity so that we know the difference between the good and bad effect of our own thoughts so that the essence and positivity of love, kindness and humility prevails globally.

Chapter 18

Every phase of life provides us with various experience which helps us to shape our thought process, character and life. It depends upon the mindset of an individual to absorb the right essence of those experience and induct the positivity of them. The external situation and association we keep also plays a part in human development. Though everyone are perfect in their own way , the intention and an honest initiative to raise one's mindset is important. As a matter of fact , our modern society has diverted itself and lost its essence of being human in nature and has voluntarily captivated itself within the darkness of patriarchy, social/ political and religious fanaticism and rigidity. Which has indeed lowered the basic values and intellectual factor in humans. Moreover, the purpose of human existence and the high morale associated with human nature has been tampered to such an extent that the definition of true happiness, bliss , love, kindness and gratitude has become obsolete from today's so called "modern lifestyle". As a result the so called "happy" and "successful" life is pregnant with the darkness of jealousy, hatred, envy, anger and lust. Though, civilization has technically advanced to great heights , but unless there is no change from within oneself the possibility of creating a healthy and loving society will be a distant dream. We need to rethink and make an honest initiative to introspect and work hard enough to develop our own self and realise that if there is an atmosphere of love, honesty, grace, humility, equality, respect and gratitude then the world will be free from any kind of hatred or jealousy for our fellow beings and we will truly be successful as humans.

Chapter 19

In today's modern and civilized world , every individual has his/her perception of leading a sober, happy and comfortable life which has a variety of materialistic paraphernalia. Few individuals are just happy to satisfy their own ego by analyzing and acknowledging their achievements by the effort they give to gather and collect things which can only provide happiness for a short period of time. Since the dawn of civilization it has been mentioned and taught by many thinkers innumerable times that one should focus on their deeds and perform their duties and be unattached with the result of it's result. Moreover, it has also been taught about the effort to achieve a certain goal in life. But as the time moved on the essence of understanding the wisdom of all those teachings by great thinkers and the initiative to catch and implementing the meaning of such teachings have been diluted with a certain degree of perverted mindset. As a matter of fact there is a lack of collective effort to know the real essence of humanity. As mentioned by a scientist a few centuries ago that every action has an equal reaction, similarly our every deed which is done with right intention to do good for everyone has a positive impact on ourselves in a long run. Any deed done with wrong intention indeed has a negative impact on our life and in our society. If we do sit back and think about it we can observe so many incidents happening around the world currently which is spreading a negative vibration all around the world. The simple reason for all these incidents is the mindset of few individual who don't have the capability of controlling their thoughts want to control the weaker section of society by their direct logic of perception about every aspect of human life. As humans we need to understand our role as an individual and the responsibility of being a perfect human. It's obvious in today's fast paced world to develop the tendency of anger, lust, envy, greed and lust. But as an individual and a part of the Divine Energy it's our responsibility to make a sincere effort to divert the negative energy arising within ourselves and lit the lamp of positivity in within ourselves to illuminate our precious life with the light of eternal love for everyone through our good deeds , thoughts and words. Which can help to make our experience in this world blissful.

Chapter 20

Human life in modern society is an outcome of various thoughts and emotions. Which is eventually alloyed with a series of assumption about leading a life of happiness, contentment, love, humility, gratitude and happiness. It's a general notion that accumulating of various objects of sensual pleasure are the source of happiness. As a result there is a lack of discipline in performing our duties as a human and also there is a lack of strong conviction to make our life an example for others to lead a life of fulfillment. Modern society claims to be highly educated and foresighted to attract a sense of positivity and everlasting abundance of wealth. But if there is a lack of honest initiative to revive our true nature and only work on the basis of knowledge which has the capability of restricting ourselves in a certain manner, then the cause of performing such duties can only give us a short term happiness. Every duty or action if done with proper intention and focus is bound to be beneficial and can be the cause of ultimate happiness and bliss. Unfortunately, the current society has been moulded in such a way that it tries to find happiness in external things and also indulging in sensual pleasures. Which can be the cause of frustration. We as an individual need to understand the fact that everyone of us have been gifted this human form of life and we need to strive and set an example for the next generation to understand the true meaning of life. The current global situation is not very pleasant , if a collective effort is made and all of us work upon ourselves to raise our consciousness in a higher level and set an example then such situations may not arise in future. Hence, it's the need of the hour to work upon ourselves and raise our thought process, build our character and have a strong faith that our will power to make this world a happier place will be accomplished.

Chapter 21

Today's fast paced society is a combination of a series of complexed perception. As human civilization has progressed technically, financially and have given an undoubted effort for globalization in every aspect , there has been a rapid slow initiative in knowing one true self. All the great thinkers, teachers and philosophers have emphasized in knowing one's true self and true meaning of life their teachings . But, in our modern and so called " educated " society the individual thought process has taken such a shape that it always tries to find a sense of happiness, fulfillment and contentment while getting indulged in sensual fulfilment. We as humans are meant to make our lives more meaningful and constructive through our actions, words and thoughts. But last few decades have portrayed the dark side of being "modern" and "educated" humans , who has the tendency to twist the essence of every positive aspect of human existence through their direct logic of perception. Only an honest effort to lit the lamp of true knowledge and understanding of true essence of human life can make a difference and make this world a better place filled with an aura of love, compassion, kindness and humanity.

Chapter 22

Human character is an outcome of it's various thoughts and perception about every aspect of life. It depends upon an individual to raise one's mindset to the heights of ecstasy or plunge into the depths of misery which is caused by the an uncontrolled and perverted mindset. In our everyday life we come across and meet many people in every phase of life. Some of them leave and carve a positive impact in our mind and soul and some are masked with an artificial approach of being our well wishers. But it needs a strong and open mind to acknowledge the true beauty of associating with good and like minded people. However, the association of like minded and good people with beautiful heart and soul is like a precious jewel which very few can afford. We need to understand that real beauty is always found in one's heart, soul, actions and intention. However, we shouldn't be judgemental and try to find true beauty within us and others so that it is an example for our future generations and a beautiful world.

Chapter 23

Human society has always been like a bouquet of collective mindset which is shaped by various experiences at different phases of life. Those experiences leave an impression in our mind and thought process but it depends upon an individual whether to get drenched in the impure puddle of negativity or to make an honest effort to raise our consciousness and absorb the rays of love, compassion, kindness and humility. Modern society has indeed excelled in every field , but the basic essence of humanity is still being challenged by the darkness of anger, lust, envy, greed, jealousy, fanaticism and superstition. As a result , there are instances of terrorism, socio-economic exploitation, physical and emotional torture of women and children, murder and racism etc. However, these instances raises a challenge and questions about our purpose of life. Though , we as humans have been able to develop our lifestyle, but unless there is no initiative to know one true self, all sort of elevated lifestyle and luxuries are of no importance. The current global situation is enveloped in a phase of high intolerance and it has also effected human psychology in various intensity. Which has indeed made a room for chaos all around us. However, all the prevailing chaos around us raises the basic question that are we justifying our existence or purpose of human life or do we deserve to call ourselves " Educated " ? Education in today's time is only a medium for transmission of information rather than making us true humans with strong character and high consciousness. So in current global, social and personal dilemma the choice remains with us that whether we wish to make this world a paradise for our future generations or make our world a hell for them and leave them to be a slave of their perverted mindset.

Chapter 24

Our world is like a bouquet of different flowers where every individual either represents flower or thorn depending upon one's own mindset or perception about shaping one's own life. Modern society is equipped with an abundance of various information about every aspect of modern and comfortable lifestyle and ways to make it luxurious, but hardly any light is shed on the ways to improvise the quality of one's own thought process. The current dilemma which is prevailing around us is indeed a mirror reflection of different thought process which is creating a friction between different ideology, which as a result is injecting a sense of anger, lust, greed, hunger for power/money and the tendency to exploit others. Though there have been many motivational quotes to change the mindset , but unless there is a sincere initiative to ignite the passion for change from within, till then the essence of humanity will be a prisoner of it's own negativity and the mind will fall prey to it's own perverted mindset and logic of perception. Which will be harmful for entire mankind. It's only a matter of giving an honest initiative to change our thoughts and every problem around the world will walk it's path towards a solution.

Chapter 25

Emotions are one of the major factor which shapes the human thought process and makes an individual act accordingly. However, it's not necessary that every action based on emotions will be beneficial for an individual. On other hand emotions are also instrumental to divert our focus from acknowledging our the importance of our basic human needs to our never ending desire to fulfill our wants. As a result in our modern society we can observe that there are many people who struggle to fulfill their wants by crossing the limits of ethics and indulging in every form of outrageous activity which includes humiliating others on the basis of caste, creed, gender, socio – economic background, skin colour or nationality. In other words emotions have the ability to change our perception towards life and it's subtle ways to know our true inner self. It depends upon us to either be a victim of our own emotional whirlpool or be a person who can divert the emotional energy for the welfare of self and others. If there is a sincere and collective effort to strain ourselves from emotional drainage and be a person of higher consciousness and firm determination to make a change in our mindset then the aura of our sincere effort can pave the path for a better world.

Chapter 26

Our modern society has been equipped with adequate information to know the possibility to express our thoughts and opinion about various aspects of life. Though there are innumerable ways to express ourselves but it depends upon an individual whether they will take a diplomatic way or to follow the path to express oneself in an unfiltered manner. Those who usually cannot take a diplomatic path of expression try to justify their path as freedom of expression. Infact , the term " Freedom of Expression " has been used by a certain section of society to portray their ideas which is a reflection of their own chaotic mindset. It's necessary to understand that our every thought, action and speech which we try to justify within the frame of " Freedom " comes with a responsibility. If we do not think, act or speak with an essence of maturity and responsibility then the outcome can have an adverse effect around us. Moreover, if we wish to see the aura of love, kindness, gratitude and happiness around us then we need to raise our consciousness and utilise our mind to understand the wisdom of life and " Free " ourselves from the clutches of egoistic approach towards life and " Free " ourselves from any thought, action or speech which cultivates a sense of false pride in any form.

Chapter 27

In every phase of human life, curiosity has been the foundation to explore the possibility of better quality of life and raise the standard of human existence. In the process of exploring the new possibilities there has been certain aspects which has been overlooked either deliberately or unknowingly. As a matter of fact in today's fast paced world , it's a necessity to work upon the quality of life by indulging in accumulating things which can only give us external happiness. But , more importantly it's necessary to work upon one's inner self and try to explore the true essence of happiness which can elevate us to a state of bliss and help us to cultivate a sense of unalloyed love for everyone around us irrespective of caste , creed , gender , skin colour , nationality or socio economic status. As the intensity of pure love will increase with right intention then the possibility of having a sense of responsibility to sustain the essence of humanity through grace, humility, kindness, and gratitude. The need of the hour is to have the right intention to invoke our true inner self so that there is an aura of positivity around us which will emit the fragrance of pure love and help to make our world a peaceful place where there is a strong bond between every human being.

Chapter 28

Human life is a bouquet of various experience based on the action and thoughts of an individual . Although our modern society is segregated on the basis of one's thought process or perception about the sense of contentment, love , gratitude or humility, but the real challenge lays in acknowledging the basic emotional needs of humans and reacting according to time , place and circumstances. But in our fast paced society basic human emotions are not being considered or acknowledged on a serious note which is indeed a threat for the emotional well being on an individual basis. As a matter of fact we as humans are blessed with a very Divine emotion of " Love " which is subtle and yet powerful to make human life and humanity get drenched in the rays of Divine Grace, peace, tranquility and bliss. But to understand the purity and to flow in this pure emotion one has to have a sense of humility, open mind and the willingness to accept this eternal truth. Life without Love is like a barren land which is parched and waiting for rain. So that life starts thriving in it and there is happiness and contentment. Similarly, the flow love in one's life with a sense of responsibility and giving a sense of happiness and contentment can make life meaningful and worth living.

Chapter 29

Every phase of life has always been instrumental to shape an individuals thought process and mindset. Based on such mindset, one paves the way of leading a certain lifestyle. Although keeping an association of like minded people is also necessary in today's modern society, but it depends upon an individual to analyze between the good and bad of keeping the company of people. As a matter of fact, current society is a mix of various type of people who emit a certain frequency of energy through their thoughts, actions and words. But it depends upon us to acknowledge our own well being and be thoughtful about ourselves and be very careful about choosing our association. Though the modern society is well read and well informed, but the existence of false ego/pride, hypocrisy, superstition and fanaticism (in any form) cannot be denied. There might be a certain section of people who are truly well informed but unfortunately in the race of acquiring all type of information, they somehow overlook to introspect and train themselves to be mindful in any situation during their lifetime. As a result, all sorts of crime are making the human society hallow of its moral values. The essence of every creation of nature has been twisted according to the mindset of a certain section of society which don't have the capability to perceive everything around them in a manner of humility. In recent time we have been informed about a very ghastly act of a person killing an individual and chopping of her body in various pieces. Such a ghastly act is a reflection of people having a savage and uncivilized mindset which cannot be rectified by any level of philosophy or argument. Such mindset is a result of false ego and a sense of superiority which is harmful for the society as a whole. It is a collective responsibility of human society to train the mind and thought process from childhood which can make an individual a better person and have a sense of gratitude, humility and kindness for other fellow beings and most importantly acknowledge the individuality of the opposite person and respecting the right to life and respect of everyone around us.

Chapter 30

Human desire to lead a life of luxury has always been a dream of most of individuals since a long time. There are indeed many instances that different people at different ages has always struggled to achieve their aspirations by any means. Few of them achieved it and had utilized it to satisfy their false pride and ego. There had been seldom any individual who took the initiative to utilize their power and resources to do something constructive for mankind. In the race of achieving and leading a luxurious lifestyle, most people have overlooked the basic humanity and have voluntarily become slaves of their senses. Those who have become the slave of their own senses have swayed away and twisted the true definition of a happy life which is in harmony with nature. People consider power, fame and money to be the foundation of a happy , successful life which can eventually lead to a luxurious life, forgetting the fact that it's only love, humility and respect for others can bring ultimate bliss in one's own life. Human life is precious and it needs to be cherished with a sense of ultimate bliss and a higher sense of purpose which can help to bring human co-operation around the world, so that unwanted commotion can be eliminated from our beautiful planet. The negativity of hatred, lust, ego, false pride are like termite which is making the humanity extinct from us humans. It's time that we need to realize our true purpose and have pure intention while we live our life fulfilling our duties.

Chapter 31

In recent years , our society has been going through a rough phase which has opened a window of opportunity to see beyond the obvious and find a solution to all the problems which are raising a question about the basic essence of humanity. It's just a matter of taking an honest initiative to understand and acknowledging our true purpose of existence. It's a matter of fact that currently our world is going through a rough phase where we are witnessing few calamities including war, disease, ideological difference between certain group of people and natural disaster. As a result there is a certain intensity of chaos and confusion . There are discussions in various platforms to find a solution and break the chain of such ongoing dilemma which drains out an individual of energy and resources. We as humans, need to acknowledge the fact that the real solution lays in giving an honest effort and eliminate the darkness of arrogance, lust, envy, anger and greed. It's time that we need to spread the essence/fragrance of love all around. So that there is harmony between people and nature.

Chapter 32

Human emotions are like a bouquet which helps us to know our true self including our strengths and weakness. We as humans are blessed with the ability to express our emotions either through words or actions. That's a major reason which makes us different from other living species. Great thinkers have always guided us to acknowledge our power to express our emotions in a subtle manner. Among all the emotions the feeling of "Love" is the most purest of emotion. It enables us express our gratitude, affection and a sense of belongingness for the opposite person. But as the wheel of time has kept rolling the basic meaning of this purest form of emotion has been twisted in a perverted manner. There has indeed been few instances in recent times which was portrayed as a gesture of Love, but it ended up with in disaster. In modern time it's necessary to introspect our true self and realign our human instinct with our true self. It's also necessary to understand that Love is the foundation of every action in our life. But it depends that whether we are using for the well being of our loved one or try to satisfy our own senses. Once the fog of ignorance is cleared from our intellect then we can understand the true meaning of Love and illuminate our life and the world.

About the Author

Karan Sharma

Karan Sharma has been self employed for last 11 years and is curious to explore the beauty of nature and the essence of human existence.

www.ingramcontent.com/pod-product-compliance
Lightning Source LLC
LaVergne TN
LVHW041558070526
838199LV00046B/2034